Grey Wolf, Prince Jack and the Firebird

Other brilliant stories to collect:

Grey Wolf, Prince Jack and the Firebird

Retold by
Alan Garner

Illustrated by
James Mayhew

SCHOLASTIC
Home of the Story

Scholastic Children's Books,
Commonwealth House, 1–19 New Oxford Street,
London WC1A 1NU, UK
a division of Scholastic Ltd
London ~ New York ~ Toronto ~ Sydney ~ Auckland
Mexico City ~ New Delhi ~ Hong Kong

First published by Scholastic Ltd, 1998

ISBN: 0 590 54389 X

Printed and bound by Cox & Wyman Ltd., Reading, Berks

2 4 6 8 10 9 7 5 3 1

Once, long ago, not near, not far, not high, not low, at the place where seven rivers meet, there lived a king. And he was the king of the Stone Castle. He had three sons, and the name of the youngest was Prince Jack.

The king had a garden, too, and round it a wall. And in the garden

there stood a tree. Gold was its trunk, and gold were its branches, gold its twigs, gold its leaves, and golden its fruit of apples. And there was never a moment when the king of the Stone Castle did not keep guards about this wondrous tree.

One night, at deep midnight, there came a music into the garden.

It was music with wings,
Trampling things, tightened strings,
Warriors, heroes, ghosts on their feet,
Boguls and boggarts, bells and snow,

That set in sound lasting sleep
The whole great world
With the sweetness of the
calming tunes
That music did play.

The next morning, the king walked in his garden, and he saw that a golden apple had been taken from the tree.

"Who has stolen my apple of gold?" said the king of the Stone Castle.

"No one," said the guard captain.
"We watched all night."

"You did not," said the king. And
he made the guards prisoners, and
sent them to work salt for ever.

"Now," said the king, "which of my
beloved sons will watch my tree? I
shall give half my kingdom now, and
all of it when I die, to the son who will
catch this thief."

"I shall watch, father," said the
oldest son. And that night he sat in
the garden, his back against the tree.

At deep midnight, at dark midnight,
there came a music over the wall.

It was music with wings,
Trampling things, tightened strings,
Warriors, heroes, ghosts on their feet,
Boguls and boggarts, bells and snow,
That set in sound lasting sleep
The whole great world
With the sweetness of the
calming tunes
That music did play.

And the oldest son slept.

The next morning, the king walked in his garden, and he saw that another golden apple had been taken from the tree.

"Who stole my apple of gold?" said the king of the Stone Castle. "Who is the thief?"

"No one, father," said the oldest son. "I watched all night."

"Then tonight I shall watch," said the second son. And the next night he sat in the garden, his back against the tree.

At deep midnight, at dark midnight, at blue midnight, there came a music into the garden.

It was music with wings,
Trampling things, tightened strings,
Warriors, heroes, ghosts on their feet,
Boguls and boggarts, bells and snow,
That set in sound lasting sleep
The whole great world
With the sweetness of the
calming tunes
That music did play.

And the second son slept.

The next morning, the king walked in his garden, and he saw that another apple had been taken from the tree.

"Who has stolen my golden apple?" said the king of the Stone Castle. "Who is the thief?"

"No one, father," said the second son. "I watched all night."

"Then I shall watch," said Prince Jack. And the next night he sat in the garden, his back against the tree. But he took his dagger and put it between his leg and the earth, the point upward, and the leg on the point.

At deep midnight, at dark mid-

night, at blue midnight, at the
midnight of all, a music came into
the garden.

It was music with wings,
Trampling things, tightened strings,
Warriors, heroes, ghosts on their feet,
Boguls and boggarts, bells and snow,
That set in sound lasting sleep
The whole great world
With the sweetness of the
calming tunes
That music did play.

And Prince Jack pushed his leg on

the dagger, and a drop of his blood fell to the earth, but he did not sleep.

Then flew the Firebird, with eyes of crystal, over the wall, over the garden, to the tree.

And Prince Jack pushed his leg on the dagger, and a second drop of his blood fell to the earth, but he did not sleep.

The Firebird perched on the lowest branch of the tree and took an apple in her beak.

Prince Jack pulled the dagger from his leg, and a third drop of his blood fell to the earth. He jumped to seize

the Firebird, but his wound made him weak, and he caught hold of a tail-feather only, and the Firebird flew away.

Prince Jack wrapped the feather in his neckcloth and sat down again beside the tree.

The next morning, the king walked in his garden, and he saw that another apple had been taken from the tree.

"Who has stolen the apple?" said

15

the king of the Stone Castle. "Who is
the thief?"

"It is the Firebird, Father," said
Prince Jack. "I did not sleep. Here are
three drops of my blood upon the
earth. And here the feather for you to
see." And he unwrapped his neckcloth, and the garden, even in that
morning, was filled with a flame of
light.

The king of the Stone Castle said,
"It is the Firebird." And he said to his
two oldest sons, "Go. I give you my
blessing. Bring the Firebird to me;
and what I promised before I shall give

to the one who brings me that Bird."

The sons took their father's blessing and rode away.

"Father, let me go, too," said Prince Jack.

"I cannot lose all my sons," said the king. And Prince Jack went to his room and he thought; and he ran to the stables, took his horse, muffled its hooves, and rode away.

He rode near and far, he rode high and low, by lanes and ways and woods and swamps, for a long time or a short time; and he came to a wide field, a green meadow, an open plain. And on the meadow stood a pillar of stone, with words graven in it.

"Go straight, know cold and hunger.
Go right, keep life, lose horse.
Go left, keep horse, lose life."

"Dear horse," said Prince Jack, and he turned to the right.
He rode one day. He rode two days.

He rode three days. Then, in a dark forest, he met a Grey Wolf.

"Did you not read the rock?" said the Grey Wolf. And he took the horse, ripped it to bits, ate it; then went.

Prince Jack walked one day. He walked two days. He walked three days. He walked until he was so tired that it could not be told in story. And the Grey Wolf came to him again.

"You are brave enough," said the Grey Wolf. "So I shall help you. I have eaten your good horse, and I shall serve you a service as payment. Sit

you up on me and say where I must take you. The roads are open to the wise, and they are not closed to the foolish."

So Prince Jack sat up on the Grey Wolf.

The Grey Wolf struck the damp earth and ran, higher than the trees, lower than the clouds, and each leap measured a mile; from his feet stones flew, springs sprouted, lakes surged and mixed with yellow sand, and forests bent to the ground. Prince Jack shouted a shout, whistled a whistle, snake and adder hissed, nightingales

sang, and beasts on chains began to roar. And the Grey Wolf stopped at a wall.

"Now, Prince Jack," he said, "get down from me, the Grey Wolf, climb over the wall, into the garden. It is the garden of the king of the Copper Castle. In the garden stand three cages. In the first cage there is a crow. In the next cage there is a jackdaw. In the golden cage there is the Firebird. Take the Firebird, put her in your neckcloth and come back. But do not, do not, do not ever take the golden cage."

Prince Jack climbed the wall, passed the first cage, passed the second cage, and put the Firebird in his neckcloth. But the golden cage was so beautiful. He picked it up, and there sounded throughout the garden and throughout that kingdom a great clang of bells and a twang of harps, and five hundred watchmen came and took him to the king of the Copper Castle.

"Why do you steal the Firebird?" said the king.

"The Firebird stole my father's golden apples," said Prince Jack. "And

he is a king."

"If you had come to me first, I should have given you the Firebird with honour," said the king of the Copper Castle. "But you came as a thief. How will it be with you now when I send through all kingdoms that your father's son brought shame within my borders?"

"The shame is great," said Prince Jack. "There is no place of honour left for me."

"Then I shall give you one chance, since you have been honest with me," said the king. "If you will ride across

thrice nine lands, beyond the Tenth
Kingdom, and get for me the Horse of
the Golden Mane, I shall give you
back your honour and, with all joy,
the Firebird, too."

The five hundred watchmen took
Prince Jack to the bounds of the gar-
den, and threw him out. The Grey
Wolf came to him.

"You did not, and you would not,
as I told you," said the Grey Wolf.
"But this is not trouble yet. The trouble is to come. I have only a trotter
and a sheep's cheek, and they must
do."

Prince Jack and the Grey Wolf ate the trotter and the sheep's cheek. Then Prince Jack sat up on the Grey Wolf, and the Grey Wolf struck the damp earth and ran, higher than the trees, lower than the clouds, and each leap measured a mile; from his feet stones flew, springs sprouted, lakes surged and mixed with yellow sand, and forests bent to the ground. Prince Jack shouted a shout, whistled a whistle,

snake and adder hissed, nightingales sang, and beasts on chains began to roar.

The Grey Wolf stopped at white-walled stables.

"Get down from me, the Grey Wolf," he said, "into the white-walled stables. They are the white-walled stables of the king of the Iron Castle. Take the Horse of the Golden Mane. But do not, do not, do not ever take the gold bridle."

Prince Jack went into the white-walled stables and took the Horse of the Golden Mane. But the gold bridle

was too beautiful to leave. He picked
it up, and thunder sounded through
the stables and five hundred grooms
came and brought him to the king of
the Iron Castle.

"Why did you steal the Horse of
the Golden Mane?" said the king.

"Because the Firebird stole my
father's golden apples," said Prince
Jack. "And he is a king. Then I stole
the Firebird, but was caught as I am
now."

"If you had come to me first, I
should have given you the Horse of
the Golden Mane with honour," said

the king of the Iron Castle. "But you came as a thief. How will it be with you now when I send through all kingdoms that your father's son brought shame within my borders?"

"The shame is great," said Prince Jack. "There is no place of honour left for me."

"Then I shall give you one chance, since you have been honest with me," said the king. "If you will ride across thrice nine lands, beyond the Tenth Kingdom, and get for me the Princess Helen the Fair, whose skin is so clear that you see the marrow flow from

bone to bone, I shall give you back your honour and, with all joy, the Horse of the Golden Mane."

The five hundred grooms took Prince Jack to the door of the white-walled stables and threw him out. The Grey Wolf came to him.

"You did not, and you would not, as I told you," said the Grey Wolf. "But this is not trouble yet. The trouble is to come. I have only a trotter and a sheep's cheek, and they must do."

Prince Jack and the Grey Wolf ate the trotter and the sheep's cheek. Then Prince Jack sat up on the Grey Wolf, and the Grey Wolf struck the damp earth and ran, higher than the trees, lower than the clouds, and each leap measured a mile; from his feet stones flew, springs spurted, lakes surged and mixed with yellow sand, and forests bent to the ground. Prince Jack shouted a shout, whistled a whistle, snake and adder hissed, nightingales sang, and beasts on chains began to roar.

The Grey Wolf stopped at the golden fence of the garden of Princess

Helen the Fair, whose marrow flowed from bone to bone.

"Get down from me, the Grey Wolf," he said. "Go back along the road by which we came, and wait for me in the field with a green oak tree." So Prince Jack did.

But the Grey Wolf, he stayed.

And, at evening, the Princess Helen the Fair came into the garden, and her marrow flowed from bone to bone. The Grey Wolf jumped into the garden, seized her, and ran off. He ran to the field of the green oak, where Prince Jack waited. Princess Helen the

Fair dried her eyes fast when she saw
Prince Jack.

"Sit up on me," said the Grey Wolf,
"and hold the princess in your arms."

Prince Jack sat up on the Grey
Wolf, and held Princess Helen the
Fair in his arms, and the Grey Wolf
ran as only a wolf runs in story, until
they came to the white-walled stables
of the king of the Iron Castle with the
Horse of the Golden Mane. But by
now Prince Jack loved Princess Helen
the Fair, and she loved him, and the
Grey Wolf saw.

"I have served you in much," said

the Grey Wolf. "I shall serve you in this. I shall be Princess Helen the Fair, and you will take me to the king, and he will give you the Horse of the Golden Mane. Then mount you the horse and ride far. And when you think of me, the Grey Wolf, I shall come to you."

And the Grey Wolf struck the damp earth, and became a False Princess, and Prince Jack took him into the white-walled stables, while Princess Helen the Fair stayed out-side.

When he saw the False Princess, the

king of the Iron Castle was pleased,
and he gave Prince Jack the Horse of
the Golden Mane with joy, and the
gold bridle, and gave him back his
honour, too. Then Prince Jack rode
out of the white-walled stables on the
Horse of the Golden Mane and put
Princess Helen the Fair before him,
and rode away.

The False Princess, the Grey Wolf,
stayed one day in the king's palace.

He stayed two days. And he stayed three. Then he asked the king if he might walk in the garden. So the king ordered serving-women to walk with the False Princess. And, as they walked, Prince Jack, far away, riding, called, "Grey Wolf! Grey Wolf! I am thinking of you now!"

The False Princess, walking in the garden with the serving-women, sprang up as the Grey Wolf, over the garden wall and ran as only wolves do in story until he came to Prince Jack.

"Sit up on me, the Grey Wolf," he said, "and let Princess Helen the Fair

ride the Horse of the Golden Mane."

And so they went on together.

At last, after a long time or a short time, they came to the palace of the king of the Copper Castle who kept the Firebird.

"Dear friend! Grey Wolf!" said Prince Jack. "You have served me many services. Serve me one more."

"I shall serve you once more," said the Grey Wolf. And he struck the damp earth and became a False Horse, and Prince Jack mounted him and rode into the palace.

When the king of the Copper

Castle saw the False Horse, he was pleased, and he gave Prince Jack the Firebird in its golden cage, and gave him back his honour, too.

Prince Jack left the palace and went to where Princess Helen the Fair was waiting with the Horse of the Golden Mane, and they rode towards the palace of Prince Jack's father, the king of the Stone Castle. They came into a dark forest.

And Prince Jack remembered, and called, "Grey Wolf! Grey Wolf! I am thinking of you now!" And straight away the Grey Wolf appeared. But he

said, "Well, Prince Jack, here is where we met. I, the Grey Wolf, have paid for your horse. I am no more your servant." And he jumped into a thicket and was gone.

Prince Jack wept, and rode the Horse of the Golden Mane, with the gold bridle, Princess Helen the Fair before him, and in her arms the Firebird and its golden cage.

They rode one day. They rode two days. They rode three days. But whether the way was long or short, they grew tired, and when they came to the graven stone in the green meadow, they rested against it, and slept.

And as they slept, the two older brothers came back from their empty wanderings, and when they saw Prince Jack with the Firebird in its golden cage, and the Horse of the Golden Mane and its gold bridle, and Princess Helen the Fair, whose marrow flowed from bone to bone, they cut Prince Jack into four pieces, and threw the four

pieces to the four winds, and took the Firebird and the Horse of the Golden Mane and Princess Helen the Fair with them back to their father's palace.

The king of the Stone Castle was glad to see his sons and to hold the Firebird in its golden cage. And the two brothers drew lots, and the first won Princess Helen the Fair, and the second took the Horse of the Golden Mane, and a wedding was ordered.

But Prince Jack lay dead, by lanes and ways and woods and swamps, out on the green meadow, cut into four parts.

He lay one day. He lay two days. He
lay three days. And, in the forest, the
Grey Wolf smelt the flesh, and knew
that it was the flesh of Prince Jack.
He went to where the pieces lay. And
there came a crow with brazen beak
and brazen claws, with her two children, to feed on the flesh. But the
Grey Wolf jumped and seized one of
her children.

"Grey Wolf, wolf's son," said the

crow, "do not eat my child. Do not tear off its rash little head. Do not take it from the bright world."

"Black Crow, crow's daughter," said the Grey Wolf, "serve me a service, and I shall not hurt your child. Fly for me over the Glass Mountains to the Well of the Water of Death and the Well of the Water of Life. Bring me back those waters, and I, the Grey Wolf, shall loose your child. But, if not, I shall tear off its rash little head. I shall take it from the bright world."

"I shall do you this service," said the crow. And she flew beyond the end

of the earth, over the Glass Mountains, and she came back with the Water of Death and the Water of Life.

The Grey Wolf tore the crow's child to bits. He sprinkled over it the Water of Death, and the bits grew together. He sprinkled over it the Water of Life, and the crow's child awoke, shook itself, and flew away.

The Grey Wolf sprinkled the pieces of the body of Prince Jack with the Water of Death. And the pieces were joined. He sprinkled the Water of Life. And Prince Jack stretched himself,

yawned, and said, "How long have I
been asleep?"

"Yes, Prince Jack, and you would
have slept for ever, had it not been for
me, the Grey Wolf. Long hair, short
wit. Sit up on me, for your oldest
brother is to wed Princess Helen the
Fair this very day."

Prince Jack sat up on the Grey
Wolf, and the Grey Wolf struck the
damp earth and ran, higher than the
trees, lower than the clouds, and each
leap measured a mile; from his feet
stones flew, springs spurted, lakes
surged and mixed with yellow sand,

and forests bent to the ground. Prince
Jack shouted a shout, whistled a whistle, snake and adder hissed, nightingales sang, beasts on chains began to
roar, all the way to the palace of the
king of the Stone Castle.

Prince Jack got down from the Grey
Wolf in the middle of the wedding,
and when she saw him alive, Princess
Helen the Fair ran to him, and they

told the king all that had happened.

The anger of the king was a river in storm, and he called halt to the wedding, made his oldest son a scullion, his second son a cowherd, and fed them all their days on cockroach milk. But Prince Jack and Princess Helen the Fair were married that same night. And on all sides those that weep were weeping, those that shout were shouting, and those that sing were singing.

Prince Jack said, "Grey Wolf! Grey Wolf! How can I repay you? Stay with me for ever. You shall never want. Go

now for ever through my ground. No
arrow will be let at you. No trap will
be set for you. Take any beast to take
with you. Go now through my ground
for ever."

"Keep your herds and your flocks to
yourself," said the Grey Wolf. "There
is many a one who has trotters and
sheep as well as you. I, the Grey Wolf,
shall get flesh without putting trouble
here. The tale is spent. Live long,
Prince Jack. Live happy. But me you
shall see never more." And the Grey
Wolf struck the damp earth and was
gone.

Prince Jack and Princess Helen the Fair lived in friendship and they lived in peace, they lived happily and they lived long; and if they are not dead yet, they are living still, and they feed the hens with stars.

But the Grey Wolf they did not see; though you may. And, if you do, what then?